My SHOES Take Me EVERYWHERE!

Claire Dulaney

Fulton Books, Inc.
Meadville, PA

Published by Fulton Books 2020

ISBN 978-1-64654-064-8 (paperback)
ISBN 978-1-64654-065-5 (digital)

Printed in the United States of America

DEDICATION

This book is dedicated to my husband, Brian, who has said "Yes, Dear" so many times. "Yes, Dear" when I wanted to start a business, change jobs, invent a new hobby, redecorate any and every part of the house, build a new house, take a trip, buy new shoes, and especially when he said "Yes, Dear" when I decided to publish a book. Thanks for all the "Yes, Dears!"

My SHOES take me EVERYWHERE!

My SHOES are big, and we pretend,

my SHOES tie, and we go to school.

My SHOES are furry, and we keep warm,

and my SHOES slip on, and
we go to the pool.

My SHOES take me EVERYWHERE!

My SHOES buckle, and we sing,

my SHOES are rubber, and we keep dry.

My SHOES are Velcro, and
we play at the park,

and my SHOES have sole,
and we jump high.

My SHOES take me EVERYWHERE!

My SHOES are dirty and worn out,

my SHOES are fancy, and we shine.

My SHOES fit only me,

Milk - 25¢
Candy -50¢
Ice Cream - 70¢
Popcorn - 80¢

and my SHOES help me stand in line.

My SHOES take me EVERYWHERE!

My SHOES are soft, and we read books,

my SHOES are tight, and we scream.

My SHOES fall off by the bed,

and my SHOES wait patiently
while we dream.

My SHOES take me EVERYWHERE!

About the Author

Claire has always loved children, books, and shoes! As a child, she loved reading Aesop's fairy tales, Mother Goose nursery rhymes, and Nancy Drew books with her mother and grandmother. If they weren't available, she read to her dolls and paper dolls. And even then, she also loved shoes, often with matching purses and hats! Professionally, she found her love in teaching children of all ages and training educators in best teaching practices. She always incorporates story time into both. A graduate of Texas Tech University, Claire and her husband, Brian, live in Lubbock, Texas. They are most proud of their two children and their spouses and their six grandsons, whom they call the "Super Six." And she's very proud of all her shoes!

CPSIA information can be obtained
at www.ICGtesting.com
Printed in the USA
BVHW061954290921
617774BV00008B/174